The Secret Tree-House

by RUTH CHEW

Illustrated by the author

SCHOLASTIC BOOK SERVICES
NEW YORK • TORONTO • LONDON • AUCKLAND • SYDNEY • TOKYO

Copyright © 1974 by Ruth Chew. All rights reserved. Published by Scholastic Book Services, a division of Scholastic Magazines, Inc.

2nd printing .... December 1974

Printed in the U.S.A.

To Hedi

1

"THAT must be the biggest pear tree in the world." Mrs. Carter put down her coffee cup and stared out of the kitchen window.

Mr. Carter reached for another pancake. "I didn't know we had a tree in our yard."

"We don't, Daddy," Elaine said. "It's in somebody else's yard."

Sam finished drinking his milk and got up from the table. "You always think you know everything, Elaine," he said to his older sister. "That pear tree isn't in anybody's yard. It's in the vacant lot in the middle."

Margaret jumped out of her chair and followed her twin brother to the window. "Oh," she said, "that's why there are two fences between us and the house at the back."

"It's a funny place for a vacant lot," Mr. Carter said. "I wonder who owns it."

"We can ask the neighbors when we get to know them better." Mrs. Carter took the milk container away from little Joey. He was trying to fill his glass. Joey was only three years old.

The Carters were having breakfast for the first time in the big old Brooklyn house. They had moved into it the day before.

Mr. Carter finished his pancake. He wiped his mouth with a paper napkin and pushed back his chair. "I'm off to the office," he said. "I want you all to help your mother get this place in order."

Margaret thought her father was glad

to go to work this morning. The house was crammed with boxes. Everything had to be put away. Margaret wished she could go with her father.

Elaine was standing at the sink. "It's your turn to wash, Margaret," she said. "I'll dry." She picked up a dish towel and stood waiting.

Sam and Margaret looked out the window at the pear tree. It was covered with enormous pears. The tree was taller than the houses in the block. The houses

were all joined together. Each one had a small, fenced-in yard. In the center was the vacant lot.

From an upstairs window Margaret had seen that there were other trees in the lot. There were tall weeds and creeping vines too. It looked like a jungle.

"Margaret," Elaine said, "hurry up with the dishes."

"Sam," Mrs. Carter called from the living room, "see if you can find the hammer. We have to hang the pictures."

"Margaret," Sam whispered. "One of the boards on the back fence is loose." Then he went to help his mother.

"What was Sam whispering about?" Elaine asked.

Margaret went to the sink and turned on the hot water. "Nothing," she said. She picked up a dish and began to wash it.

2

BY late afternoon everything was put away. Margaret and Sam slipped out the back door into the summer sunshine.

Sam tugged at the wide gray board on the fence. It pulled away from the cross bar that ran along the back. Now the board was only held by one big nail. Sam used the nail as a kind of hinge. He swung the board to one side.

Margaret slid through the opening in the fence into the vacant lot on the other side. Sam came after her. He let the fence board swing back into place behind him.

The twins looked around. The lot was littered with piles of old bricks overgrown with weeds. Clumps of tall hollyhocks grew wild. There were three of the fern-like weed trees that grow everywhere in Brooklyn. Over everything was a tangle of Virginia creeper and wild grapevines.

The pear tree grew in the middle of the lot. Margaret and Sam made their way through the vines and over the piles of bricks until they reached the big tree. Sam pulled himself up onto the lowest branch. He reached over his head and picked a huge pear — the biggest pear that Sam had ever seen.

Margaret climbed up beside Sam. She sat on the branch and swung her feet. "Give me a bite, Sam," she said.

"You can have half." Sam took his pen knife out of his pocket and started to cut the pear. "This is kind of a hard pear," he said. Sam sawed through the pear.

Margaret took half the pear and tried to bite into it. "Ow! It sure is hard. I almost broke a tooth." Margaret looked at the pear. The seeds in the middle were dark and shiny. Margaret dug three large pointed seeds out of the pear and put them into the pocket of her jeans.

"What did you do that for?" Sam asked.

"I don't know. I just like the way they look." Margaret stared up into the thick branches over her head.

With his knife Sam cut out a seed from his half of the pear. He dropped it into his shirt pocket. Then he wiped his knife on his pants leg and put it away.

"Why don't we build a tree-house?" Margaret said.

"Elaine could see it." Sam pointed to Elaine's window. "Or else Mom would spot it from the kitchen. Either way

Mom would say it wasn't safe. And she'd make us stay out of the lot."

Margaret looked down. There was a hollow in the ground at the foot of the pear tree. "A cave! Why don't we dig a cave?"

Sam pointed to a pile of bricks. "We could prop up the walls with those," he said. "Come on, Mag. Let's get started."

Margaret and Sam climbed down from the tree. Margaret began to scoop out dirt with her hands. Sam broke a small branch off one of the weed trees. He jabbed it into the ground.

Margaret was surprised to find how easy it was to dig with her hands. Soon the hole was so deep that she and Sam had to get into it. When they couldn't see over the edge they began to tunnel under the tree. They piled the dirt they dug out around the edge of the hole.

"I always thought it would be much

harder than this to dig a cave," Sam said. "It's almost as if it's digging itself."

Margaret put down the handful of dirt she had scraped from the ground. She stared at the hollow under the tree. "Sam," she whispered, "look! It *is* digging itself!"

The cave was getting bigger and bigger without their doing anything at all. The dirt wasn't coming out or piling up, but the cave under the tree looked deep and shadowy now. And it was getting bigger all the time.

3

FOR a minute Sam and Margaret just looked at each other. Then Sam started to climb out of the hole. "Let's go home, Mag."

Margaret grabbed Sam's arm. "I know how you feel," she said. "It's scary, but I want to see what's inside the cave."

"Suppose it keeps getting bigger and bigger," Sam said. "We might never get out."

"We won't go that far in," Margaret promised. She stuck her head into the opening of the cave. At first Margaret couldn't see a thing. Then her eyes began to get used to the darkness. "It's not very big at all." Margaret stepped into the cave.

Sam came in after her. The roof of the cave was formed by the roots of the pear tree. The tree roots crawled down the walls too. They seemed to hold the dirt in place. The cave was more round than square. And it had a lumpy floor. The air inside was cool and fresh. A little breeze seemed to come from somewhere.

Margaret thought she saw a dim light high overhead. She grabbed a root that hung down the wall and climbed toward the light.

"What are you doing, Mag?" Sam wanted to know.

Margaret could hear a rustling far above. "I've got to find out what's up there." She climbed higher.

Sam felt the root Margaret was climbing. It was thick and twisted and sturdy as the trunk of a young tree. "I'm coming too." Sam swung himself up after his twin sister.

Before long the root came to an end. It just joined itself to the wall. Now Sam and Margaret found that they were in a sort of well. Knobs stuck out of the sides of the well. Margaret used them as a stair, grabbing one knob with her hands and putting her foot on another. It was exciting. Margaret climbed higher and higher. Sam was right behind her.

The light was brighter now, and the rustling sounded like the leaves of a tree. At last Margaret came to an opening in the side of the well. It was like a round window. She looked out.

Something fierce and furry dived at Margaret's face. She drew back from the window so fast that she almost fell. Sam grabbed one of her ankles to steady her. Then he climbed up to where he could see out of the opening too.

An angry gray squirrel sat on a branch beside a great green pear. It looked at Margaret with bright eyes and chattered at her in a rage.

"Look, Mag." Sam pointed to a big untidy nest nearby. In it were three fuzzy little squirrels.

"Oh," Margaret said. "That's why she's so mad. She thinks I'm after them." She looked at the squirrel. "I won't hurt your babies."

The squirrel made a few more fierce remarks and then moved over to her nest. She kept a sharp eye on the hole in the tree trunk.

"We climbed up inside the pear tree," Sam said. "You wanted a tree-house, Mag. This is a cave *and* a tree-house, a secret tree-cave."

4

MARGARET and Sam were so high in the tree that they could see into all the yards in the block. A cat was walking along the fence between the Carters' house and the next one.

"That's Blackie," Sam said. "He belongs to Mrs. Jenkins, the old lady who lives next door."

At this moment Mrs. Jenkins came out of her back door. She made little hissing noises to call the cat. Blackie jumped off the fence and ran over to her. Mrs. Jenkins bent over and picked him up.

When she stood up again she seemed to look right at the pear tree. Sam and Margaret were leaning out of the hole in the trunk. They pulled back inside the tree.

"Do you think she saw us?" Margaret asked.

"I hope not. She might tell Mom." Sam began to climb down inside the tree. His foot slipped off one of the knobs. Sam skidded part of the way down. He stiffened his back and pressed his hands and feet against the inside of the tree trunk. "Next time we climb up here I'm going to bring a rope."

When they reached the bottom of the tree trunk the twins grabbed hold of the root and lowered themselves to the floor of the cave.

"We'd better get home before Mom starts looking for us," Margaret said. She stepped out of the cave and climbed to the top of the hole. Sam followed her.

They made their way through the weeds and over the piles of broken bricks to their back fence. Sam was looking for the loose board. Suddenly he heard Elaine's voice from the other side of the fence. "The twins aren't out here, Mother."

Sam and Margaret stopped still where they were. Sam looked through a crack between the boards.

The Carters' yard was a patch of trampled grass. A tall hollyhock that had gone to seed leaned against the fence near the back door. And a few raggedy clumps of blue dayflowers grew here and there. A narrow concrete walk went around the little yard, about three feet from the fence. Close to the house the concrete was wider. Elaine had brought a card table out of the house and set it up on the concrete.

Mrs. Carter was putting plates on the table. Little Joey was helping by carrying out the spoons and forks.

"We're going to have a picnic in the yard," Sam whispered.

Suddenly Margaret knew that she was going to sneeze. She held her breath and felt in her pocket for a piece of Kleenex. Her fingers touched something hard and pointed — a pear seed. At once the sneeze feeling was gone. Margaret took the pear seed out of her pocket to look at it.

She held the seed between her thumb and forefinger. Her thumbnail was pressed against it. The seed cracked. Margaret stared at it. "Sam," she said in a low voice, "it's growing!"

Sam looked. The shiny brown seed got bigger and bigger until Margaret had to hold it with two hands. Then a beak poked out of the crack in the seed. A

minute later the seed opened wide. A
shiny green bird with a long tail hopped
out. It cocked a bright eye at the two
children. Then it flapped its wings and
flew over the fence into the yard.

Sam peeked between two fence
boards. He saw Elaine and Mrs. Carter
setting the table. The bird swung twice
around the table and then flew through

the open back door into the house. Joey dropped the spoons and forks on the ground and ran into the house after the bird.

"Mother," Elaine yelled, "if it bites him he'll get parrot fever."

Mrs. Carter put down the plates and went into the house. Elaine picked up the spoons and forks and followed her mother.

"Quick!" Sam swung the loose board to one side. He and Margaret slipped through the fence into the yard and pushed the board back into place.

Mrs. Carter came out of the back door. "Oh, here you are," she said to the twins. "Did either of you see a green bird fly out of the house? We saw it go in, but we can't find it anywhere inside."

"There's no green bird out here, Mom," Sam said. "We'll help you look for it. Come on, Mag."

5

WHEN Mr. Carter came home, everyone was still looking for the green bird.

"It was a parrot," Mrs. Carter said. "It must have escaped from a pet shop."

"Or maybe it belongs to one of the neighbors," Mr. Carter said. "I'm hungry. Let's have supper now and look for the bird afterward."

While the Carters were picnicking, Mrs. Jenkins came out into her yard. Mr. Carter got up from the table and walked to the fence. "Mrs. Jenkins," he said, "my family saw a green parrot in the yard. Did you lose one?"

"Parrot?" Mrs. Jenkins said. "I don't own a parrot." She leaned over and pulled a dandelion out of her marigold bed. "But if there's a parrot around here he's sure to be after my sunflower seeds."

She pointed to a row of tall sunflowers growing by her fence. Some of the huge flowers had gone to seed.

After supper Margaret and Elaine were busy doing the supper dishes. Sam was helping his father put a washer in one of the faucets in the bathroom. Joey sneaked into Margaret's room. He wanted to play with her jacks. The door to the closet was open a little. Joey grabbed the handle and pulled. He heard a loud squawk. An angry bunch of green feathers bounced down from the top of the door. Joey ran screaming to his mother.

Mrs. Carter was in her bedroom reading the newspaper. "What's the matter, Joey?"

"Bird!" Joey howled.

Mrs. Carter went to look. She found the green bird perched on the banister rail at the top of the stairs. Just as she was about to swoop down and catch it in the newspaper, the bird said, "Stop that nonsense!"

Mrs. Carter dropped the newspaper. "A talking parrot!" she said.

"Awk," the bird answered.

The bathroom was just a few steps down the hall. Sam and his father left the wash basin and came to see what was going on.

"So this is the bird who's been causing all the excitement," Mr. Carter said.

"He talks, John," Mrs. Carter told him. "You're right. He must be somebody's pet."

Mr. Carter reached for the bird. "Pretty Polly."

The bird half closed its eyes and looked pleased. Then it marched along the banister rail and up Mr. Carter's arm. It perched on his shoulder.

Mr. Carter went downstairs to the kitchen to show Elaine and Margaret. "Look at my friend here," he said.

"Daddy," Elaine warned him. "Be careful he doesn't bite you."

"He won't if I feed him," Mr. Carter said. He fished a quarter out of his pocket. "Margaret, run next door and tell Mrs. Jenkins we found the parrot. Ask her if she'll sell us some of her sunflower seed."

Margaret took the quarter and went to ring Mrs. Jenkins's doorbell.

When Mrs. Jenkins saw who was outside she opened the door wide. "You're the little girl from next door," she said. "Come in."

Margaret walked into the house. It was a lot like the one the Carters had moved into. The floors and woodwork were the same, but there were heavy curtains and lamps with fringes on the shades. Something rubbed against Margaret's leg. It was the black cat. Margaret reached down to stroke him. Blackie purred.

"Sit down." Mrs. Jenkins pointed to a big easy chair.

Margaret sank so far into the soft chair that she wondered if she'd ever be able to get out. The cat jumped onto her lap.

"What's your name?" Mrs. Jenkins said. "Do you like sour balls?" She held out a jar of the hard candy.

"Thank you." Margaret took a red sour ball. "My name is Margaret. Daddy asked me to tell you we found the parrot, but we don't have anything to feed it. Please would you sell us some of your sunflower seeds?"

Mrs. Jenkins looked at her cat. "A parrot," she said. "What do you think of that, Blackie?"

The old lady hummed for a minute. Then she seemed to remember. "Sunflower seeds. Come into the garden, Margaret."

Mrs. Jenkins took a pair of shears out of her kitchen drawer. She led Margaret down a short flight of steps to her back door.

The garden was dark, but overhead a pale new moon was shining in the Brooklyn sky. Margaret followed Mrs. Jenkins to where the sunflowers grew against the fence. Mrs. Jenkins stood on tiptoe to snip the round head of seeds off the tallest plant.

"Here you are, Margaret," she said.

Margaret took the quarter out of her pocket.

"No, no." Mrs. Jenkins shook her head. "It's a gift. I'm glad to be able to help you."

6

THE parrot wouldn't eat the sunflower seeds after all. Joey pulled a long black seed out of the sunflower head and threw it at the bird. The parrot dodged, and the seed bounced off the wall.

"Why would a bird who hatched out of a seed want to eat seeds?" Sam whispered to Margaret.

Mr. Carter held a sunflower seed on the palm of his hand and made chirping noises. The parrot walked away across the kitchen table. "Well, what would you like?" Mr. Carter snapped.

"Hot buttered toast," the bird said.

Mr. Carter stared. "He's just mimicking," he said. "He doesn't know what he says."

Sam dropped a slice of bread into the toaster, and Margaret went to get a knife for the butter.

"We should put an ad in the Lost and Found column of the newspaper," Mrs. Carter said. She took the butter out of the refrigerator. "If someone can describe this parrot we'll know he's the owner. Meantime we ought to give the bird a name. What about *Caesar*?"

The toast was ready now. Margaret buttered it and gave it to the parrot. It stood on one foot and held the slice of toast with the other. "My name is Polly." The parrot took a little bite of toast.

"Pretty Polly," Mr. Carter said.

The parrot tipped her head to one side and went on eating.

Mr. Carter was shaking the sunflower seeds into an empty peanut butter jar. He cracked a seed and ate it. "Hey, these things are good."

Margaret felt the two pear seeds in her pocket. Would they too hatch parrots? She thought one parrot was enough. Margaret left the seeds where they were.

Polly had eaten most of the toast. She dropped what was left on the table. Then she flapped her wings and fluttered up onto the top of the kitchen cabinet.

Elaine looked up at the bird. "She's pretty," she said, "and so far she hasn't bitten anybody. Do you think we could keep her?"

"Of course," Mr. Carter said. "She's a wonderful bird. I never before heard a parrot talk so clearly."

Joey clapped his hands. "We have a parrot! We have a parrot!" he chanted.

Mrs. Carter frowned. "We ought to try to find her owners. They must be very unhappy to lose a bird like this."

"All right," Mr. Carter said. "Put an ad in the *Times* for three days. If nobody claims her we'll call her ours. Right, Pretty Polly?"

"Awk," said the bird.

7

MRS. Carter was putting Joey to bed in the room he shared with Sam. Sam went into Margaret's room to talk to her.

"I don't understand," Sam said. "How could a bird that came out of a pear seed talk and have a name like *Polly*? It's crazy."

"Of course, it's crazy," Margaret said. "But what about the cave that dug itself? It's all crazy, Sam."

Sam took the pear seed out of his pocket and put it on Margaret's bed. "I wonder if this one is magic too."

The twins stared at the dark pointed seed. It didn't do anything. It just lay there. Sam put it back into his pocket.

Someone was scratching at Margaret's door. She went to open it.

The green parrot walked into the room. "Oh, here you are," she said. The bird hopped up onto Margaret's bed and perched on the pillow. She looked around. "This is a nice room, but I wish you'd keep that little boy out of it."

"You mean Joey?" Sam asked. "What's the matter with him?"

"I was minding my own business, taking a nap up there." The bird nodded toward the top of the closet door. "He pulled the door out from under me. I nearly had a nasty fall." The parrot shuddered. "And now, when I went back to finish that tasty piece of toast, he grabbed it away. Then he stroked my wings with buttery fingers. I can't fly with grease on my feathers. I've been walking all over this big house looking for you."

"Poor Polly!" Margaret picked up the bird and carried her to the bathroom. Sam came along. "Rub some soap on a washcloth," Margaret said.

"Joey was only trying to make friends," Sam told the parrot.

"He didn't mean to hurt you," Margaret said.

Sam helped Margaret wash the butter off the parrot's wings. "Do you want to be dried?" He picked up a bath towel.

Polly perched on the rim of the wash basin and shook herself. "No need," she said. "I'll be all right now." She fluttered up into the air and winged her way down the hall to Margaret's room. Margaret and Sam came after her.

Margaret climbed on her chair to clear a space on the shelf of her closet for the bird. Polly settled down between Margaret's blue straw hat and her seashell collection.

"Good night," the bird said. "See you in the morning." She tucked her head under her wing.

8

FOR the next few days Sam and Margaret looked for a chance to sneak back into the lot. There were all sorts of jobs to be done around the house. When they were free it seemed as if somebody was always watching. One time they got all ready to go. Then Mrs. Carter started to shake a mop out of an upstairs window. Another time, just as they were going to shove the loose board aside, Elaine came out into the yard. She wanted to look over Mrs. Jenkins's fence and admire the sunflowers.

Nobody came to claim the parrot. The Carters were having breakfast in the kitchen. Mrs. Carter gave Sam a helping of scrambled eggs. "I guess we can call Polly our own," she said.

"We ought to keep that bird in a cage," Elaine said. "She's always taking things from my room. I haven't seen my doll's telephone for two days. And this morning the shoelace was gone from one of my sneakers."

Polly was swinging back and forth on the cord to the venetian blind. She looked at Elaine. "Fusspot!"

Joey jumped out of his chair and ran over to the parrot.

"Awk!" The bird climbed higher up the venetian blind cord. She looked out of the window. Outside Mrs. Jenkins's cat Blackie was sitting on the fence between the two yards. "Meow," the parrot said through the open window.

Blackie stood up. His tail fluffed to twice its usual size. The hair stood up on his back. He looked around for the cat who was insulting him. Then he caught sight of the parrot in the window.

"Meow," Polly repeated.

Blackie's tail returned to its normal size, but now the end of it twitched. The cat flattened his back and his green eyes gleamed.

Sam looked out of the window. "Mrs. Jenkins's cat looks as if he'd like to eat Polly."

Mr. Carter said, "I'm sure he would. You'd better keep Polly in the house. Maybe Elaine is right. We ought to get a cage."

Joey climbed up on a chair to reach for the parrot. Polly let go of the venetian blind cord and flew up onto the molding over the door.

"Sit down, Joey," Margaret said. "Polly's afraid you'll put butter on her wings. Daddy, Polly wouldn't be happy in a cage."

The parrot flew down and perched on Mr. Carter's shoulder. She gave him a little peck on the cheek.

Mr. Carter buttered a piece of toast and handed it to the bird. "Well, be careful that the cat doesn't get to her." He finished eating his eggs. "I'm off to the office," he said.

9

SAM found a coil of clothesline in a corner of the basement. He hid the rope under his shirt and went to look for Margaret.

She was in the yard. Mrs. Jenkins's cat Blackie was sitting in his favorite spot on the fence. Margaret was scratching him behind the ears. Blackie purred.

"Come on, Mag, while nobody's looking." Sam shoved the fence board to one side. Margaret left the cat and followed Sam into the lot.

The cat walked along the fence between the yards till he came to the fence at the rear. Then he sat down again and watched the children.

"Do you have your pear seed with you, Sam?" Margaret asked. "I'm keeping mine with me for luck."

"More than luck," Sam said. "They're magic."

The sun was hot. The lot seemed more like a jungle than ever. The twins made their way through the hollyhocks and the weeds to the foot of the pear tree. They jumped down into the hole and went into the cave. It was dark and cool inside.

Sam and Margaret sat on the floor of

the cave. It felt great to be alone in their own secret hiding place. Then Sam began to climb the root up into the pear tree. Margaret was right behind him. It was much easier to climb now that they knew how.

When they came to the hole in the tree trunk Sam crawled out onto a branch of the pear tree. He tied one end of the rope to the branch and pushed the rest of the rope back through the hole into the hollow trunk. "That should make it easier going down," he said.

Margaret pulled herself out of the hole. She sat on a branch and listened to a breeze rustle the leaves around her. After a few minutes she crawled over to the squirrel's nest to look at the little squirrels. They were bigger than when Margaret had first seen them. The nest was crowded.

"Watch out, Mag! The mother squirrel

is coming." Sam climbed two branches higher in the tree.

Margaret backed away from the nest. The squirrel was leaping from branch to branch in one of the weed trees nearby. She gave a jump and landed on a twig near the nest. The branch shook so that the little squirrels nearly fell. The mother squirrel chattered and screamed at her young. Then she grabbed one of them and pulled it half out of the nest.

Margaret climbed onto the branch above. "I'll go away," she said to the squirrel. "I didn't mean to scare you. Don't make your babies leave home."

The squirrel only screamed and went on tugging at her young.

Then Margaret looked down.

At the foot of the pear tree was a huge black cat. Now Margaret knew what the squirrel was afraid of. "Sam," Margaret yelled, "look!"

Sam had been climbing higher in the tree. He didn't seem to hear. "Come on up here, Mag," he called.

Margaret scrambled onto the next branch. By the time she reached Sam, they were so high up that it made her dizzy to look down. She grabbed Sam by the arm. "Look at that cat down there," she said.

When Sam saw the cat it had started to climb the tree. "Mag," Sam said, "that's a black leopard or a puma!"

The big black cat was slowly, surely, climbing from branch to branch, coming nearer to the children.

Margaret started to climb higher. Then she stopped. "We have to go *down*, Sam. We've got to get to the hole in the trunk."

Sam nodded. His face was white. Margaret knew he was just as scared as she was. But Sam began to climb down toward the place where they had come out of the tree trunk. Margaret came after him. Her hands were sweating, and she almost lost her grip. Every step she went down brought her nearer to the cat. He was climbing silently. Now Margaret could see the gleam of his green eyes.

Sam came to the hole first, but he waited for Margaret. As soon as she was within reach, he grabbed her and pushed her into the tree trunk. "Get the rope, Mag." He crowded in after her.

The twins climbed down inside the tree. They were in such a hurry that they scraped their knees, but the rope was a help. When they reached the ground they rushed from the cave and climbed out of the hole at the foot of the tree. They stumbled over the piles of bricks and through the weeds to the loose board in their back fence.

10

MARGARET shoved the board aside and crawled into the yard. She held the board for Sam to come through.

Mrs. Jenkins was in her yard. She was weeding her aster bed. When Sam and Margaret burst through the space in their back fence the old lady looked up. She caught sight of the huge cat in the pear tree. "Oh, my goodness! Quick, go into the house, children," she said. "I'll telephone the police."

Sam and Margaret dashed in their back door and raced through the house to the living room. Elaine and Joey were sitting on the floor building a castle with Joey's blocks. Polly perched on top of the archway to the dining room. The bird held a curved block in her claws.

"Give it back, Polly," Elaine begged. "We can't build the drawbridge without it." She looked at the twins. "What's the matter?"

"There's a puma in the pear tree," Margaret gasped.

Mrs. Carter was coming down from upstairs. "Oh, is that what that is? I saw something from the window, but I don't have my glasses on, and I couldn't tell what it was." Mrs. Carter ran to the telephone and dialed. "This is an emergency," she said into the phone. "Get me the police."

In a few minutes a police car arrived with two policemen in it. They rang both the Carters' doorbell and Mrs. Jenkins's.

The two policemen were asking the neighbors for a ladder to get over the back fence. Then a van arrived with a man from the Prospect Park zoo. He rang the Carters' bell. "The police department sent for me," he told Mrs. Carter.

The zoo man went into the Carters' backyard. Margaret, Sam, Elaine, Joey, and their mother watched him from the kitchen window. Polly swung on the venetian blind cord and watched too.

The big black cat was climbing down from the pear tree. Before the zoo man knew what was happening, the cat had reached the ground. It ran to Mrs. Jenkins's back fence and jumped over it into her yard.

"Meow," the cat said in a very loud voice.

The zoo man was holding a big net. He tossed the net over the fence onto the cat. It jumped and tore at the net with its claws. But the net was strong, and the cat was caught.

The zoo man climbed the fence into Mrs. Jenkins's yard. "Funniest looking puma I ever saw," he said.

11

NEXT morning at breakfast Mr. Carter showed the family a picture of the big cat on page four of the newspaper. Polly perched on his shoulder and craned her neck to look. "No one seems to know where the cat came from," Mr. Carter said. "They're keeping it at the Prospect Park zoo."

After breakfast Margaret told Sam, "I'll bet if we didn't have the lucky pear seeds, the puma would have caught us."

Sam checked to make sure he still had his pear seed. Margaret's two seeds were safe in her pocket. They decided to climb the pear tree again. "I want to see if the baby squirrels are all right," Margaret said.

Mrs. Jenkins called to the twins when they came out into their yard. "Have you seen Blackie? He's been missing since yesterday."

"No," Margaret told her, "but I'll look for him." She went back into the house. She thought the parrot might know where the cat was. The bird was always watching him from the kitchen window. She seemed to love to tease him.

Mrs. Carter was in the kitchen.

"Where's Polly?" Margaret asked.

"Look in Elaine's room," her mother suggested.

Margaret found the parrot in Elaine's closet. She was pulling the pearl beads off the collar of Elaine's new party dress.

"Stop that, Polly!" Margaret grabbed the bird and yanked her out of the closet. "Why are you so bad?"

"I'm bored," the parrot said. "How would you like to be shut up in an old house? It's summertime. I want to fly around outside."

"Come on then." Margaret started downstairs. "Sam and I are going to climb the pear tree. But first, do you know where Blackie is?"

"Of course I know," Polly said. "There's so much talk around this place that I couldn't help knowing."

"What do you mean? Where is he?" Margaret demanded.

The parrot cocked her head. "He's all right," she said. "There's nothing wrong with that stupid cat that a cracked pear seed can't fix. And meantime I can have a little fun outdoors without having to worry about him sneaking up behind me."

"What are you talking about?" Margaret said. "Where's Blackie?"

"I told you he's all right." The parrot flapped away from Margaret and flew downstairs. Margaret ran after her.

Mrs. Carter was busy trying to pull up a venetian blind in the living room.

Sam was still in the yard. He opened the back door and yelled, "Hurry up, Mag."

Polly saw her chance. She flew over Sam's head, out of the door, and into the open air. When Margaret reached the

back door the bird was already perched high in the branches of one of the weed trees. Polly squawked at the sparrows and starlings around her.

"We'll never be able to get her down from there," Sam said. "That tree's not strong enough for us to climb."

"Maybe we can persuade her to come into the pear tree." Margaret ran to the back fence and shoved the loose board aside so she could crawl through.

Sam didn't have time to get through the fence. He was still in the yard when Elaine came out of the house. He turned his back to the fence and reached behind himself to pull the board back into place.

"Mother's looking for you, Sam," Elaine said. "She wants you to help her untangle the venetian blind cords. She can't work the blinds. That parrot has tied every cord in the house in knots."

Sam had to go into the house.

12

MARGARET decided to try to catch Polly all by herself. She made her way over to the pear tree, jumped down into the hole at the foot of it, and went into the cave.

The clothesline was still dangling down through the hollow tree overhead. Margaret took hold of the rope and swung herself onto the root that hung down into the cave.

Margaret climbed the root and then shinnied up the rope inside the tree. In almost no time she reached the hole in the trunk.

When she poked her head out of the hole Margaret looked at the squirrel's nest. It was empty. Oh dear! Margaret thought. The puma must have gotten the baby squirrels.

Then she saw the squirrels. The three little ones were sitting on a branch while their mother gave them lessons in climbing and leaping.

Margaret stayed very quiet and watched the squirrels. She put her hand in her pocket and touched a pear seed. It was cool and slippery. Margaret rubbed the seed. Suddenly she found that

she understood everything the mother squirrel was teaching her children.

It wasn't words that she understood. It was action. Margaret's body seemed to know just how to balance on one branch and how to spring into the air and grab hold of another branch. She even felt as if she had an invisible tail that would lift her like a sail in the wind.

Margaret crawled out of the trunk onto a branch. The mother squirrel looked at her and went right on teaching her babies.

The green parrot was sitting on a slender branch of the weed tree next to the pear tree. She cocked a sassy eye at Margaret.

"Polly," Margaret called. "Come over here."

"Oh no," the bird answered. "You'd only catch me and take me back into the house."

"Don't you like living with us?" Margaret asked.

"Well, I must say the food at your place is OK." Polly flew over to one of the baby squirrels and pulled its tail. The little squirrel let out a scream and nearly fell from the tree. The mother squirrel dived at the parrot.

Polly dodged her and flew back to the weed tree. "This is almost as much fun as teasing your sister," she said to Margaret.

Margaret was angry. She walked on all fours along her branch until she came as close as she could to the weed tree. Then she gave a jump and sailed through the air. She grabbed the parrot with one hand and with the other tried to get hold of a branch of the weed tree. The branch slipped out of her hand. Margaret fell, still holding onto the bird.

Margaret's shirt caught on a twig. Her

sleeve was ripped half off, but it slowed her fall.

"Help!" the bird squawked.

Margaret's feet touched a branch. She gave a spring and leaped back into the pear tree. There she landed on a strong branch and ran along it until she was close to the trunk.

"Are you out of your mind, Margaret?" the parrot asked.

Margaret didn't answer. She just ran down the trunk like a squirrel. She carried Polly home and took her into the house. She put the parrot in the bathroom and shut the door. "You can come out when you promise to be good," she told the bird.

Then she went to look for Sam.

13

ELAINE was coming up the stairs when Margaret started down. "Margaret, what happened to your sleeve?"

Margaret looked down at her polo shirt. "Yipe," she said. "Mom will be mad."

Elaine pulled at the sleeve. "It's just the seam. Come into my room. Maybe I can fix it for you."

Margaret followed Elaine to her bedroom. She took off her shirt and gave it to her sister to mend. Then she sat down on the bed. Elaine took a little sewing basket out of her dresser drawer.

"Elaine," Margaret said. "I shut Polly in the bathroom to punish her."

Elaine threaded a needle. "Don't be silly, Margaret. The parrot doesn't understand. We'll just have to get a cage for her to keep her out of trouble."

Margaret watched Elaine working on her polo shirt. Her sister wasn't a bad kid, she thought. The trouble was that she tried to be too good. "Elaine," Margaret said, "Polly's not an ordinary parrot. She does know what you say."

Elaine pricked her finger. She stuck it in her mouth. When she took it out, she said, "I know she seems to understand, but of course she can't." Elaine went on sewing.

Margaret tried again. "I know more about Polly than you think I do, Elaine. I even know where she came from."

Elaine put down the shirt. "You should have told Mother and Daddy."

"They'd never believe me," Margaret said. "I'm not sure you will."

Elaine picked up the shirt and started sewing again. "All right," she said. "Where did Polly come from?"

"She hatched out of a pear seed," Margaret said.

"A pear seed?" Elaine asked in a choked voice.

"Yes, one like this." Margaret took a pear seed out of her pocket to show her sister. "The seed got bigger and bigger. Then a green bird came out of it."

Elaine couldn't stand it any longer. She had to laugh. She could hardly finish sewing the shirt. "Margaret, how can you dream up such things? Tell Joey. He'll love that story. Here's your shirt. And try not to be such a roughneck."

Margaret put the pear seed back into her pocket and pulled on her polo shirt. "Thanks, Elaine. But please just leave the parrot where she is for a while," she begged.

14

"WHAT do you mean, you feel like a squirrel?" Sam asked.

The twins were in Margaret's room. "Look." Margaret sprang from her dresser to a chair.

"Take it easy!" Sam grabbed the chair to steady it.

Margaret took Sam outside in the yard to show him. She jumped to the top of the fence and ran along it. Sam had to admit that she was like a squirrel.

Margaret told him how she had watched the squirrel teaching her young. "Maybe if we climb the tree and you watch the mother squirrel you'd get the hang of it," Margaret said. She jumped off the back fence into the lot.

Sam pushed the loose board aside and came through.

Margaret leaped over the bricks and scampered up into the pear tree. Sam went into the cave and climbed up inside the tree. Margaret was already waiting outside the hole in the trunk when Sam got to it.

He leaned out of the hole. "Where are the squirrels?"

The children couldn't see the squirrels anywhere. Then Margaret remembered the pear seeds. "I was rubbing a pear seed when I watched the mother squirrel," she said. "Do you suppose that had anything to do with it?"

"Maybe," Sam said. He took out his pear seed and looked at it. Then he put it back into his pocket. "Why don't we go to the park? There are a lot of squirrels there. I could watch them."

Margaret saw her mother come out

into the backyard. "Hide, Sam." Margaret dived into the hole in the pear tree.

Sam looked out of the hole. "Hey, Mag, have you noticed there aren't any more pears on the tree?"

"The birds must have eaten them," Margaret said. "We'd better take care of the seeds." She began to climb down the rope inside the tree.

Margaret let go of the end of the clothesline and dropped to the floor of the cave. I̅ neakers touched something soft and wiggly. Margaret put both hands over her mouth to keep from screaming. She jumped to the side of the cave.

A long slimy shape stretched across the cave. "Sam," Margaret gasped. "There's a snake down here."

Sam clung to the root. "Don't move, Mag."

The two children watched the strange

smooth snake. Their eyes were getting used to the darkness.

"It's *pink*," Margaret whispered, "and it doesn't seem to have any eyes."

"That's no snake, Mag," Sam said. "It's a giant angleworm."

The big worm began to make a hole in the ground. Twisting and turning, it wiggled its way into the dirt.

Sam and Margaret left the cave. Their mother had gone back into the house. They found her in the living room.

Mrs. Carter was looking through the yellow pages of the telephone book. "I wonder what parrot cages are listed under," she said. "Polly got into the bathroom. She squeezed all the toothpaste out of the tube and threw the towels into the bathtub. How in the world did that bird learn to turn on faucets?"

15

THE next day Sam and Margaret asked
their mother if they could have a picnic
in the park. Mrs. Carter let them make
their own sandwiches. She gave them a
box of cookies, two cans of lemon soda,
and four peaches. "Just be sure you put
your trash into a waste basket," she said.

The twins went out the front door.
Mrs. Jenkins was walking slowly along
the sidewalk. She was looking in all the
yards and making little hissing noises.
Sam and Margaret ran down the block.
"Hello, Mrs. Jenkins," Margaret said
when they came to the old lady.

Mrs. Jenkins turned to see who had spoken to her. "Oh, hello, Margaret."

Margaret thought Mrs. Jenkins looked as if she had been crying. "What's the matter, Mrs. Jenkins?"

Now the old lady really was crying. "Blackie still hasn't come home," she said. "I'm afraid he's been run over by a car."

Margaret remembered that Polly told her the cat was all right. And the parrot seemed to know. "Oh, no," Margaret said. "Blackie's all right. I'm sure he's all right. Don't worry, Mrs. Jenkins."

Mrs. Jenkins dabbed her eyes with a piece of Kleenex. "Do you really think so, Margaret?"

Margaret nodded. Mrs. Jenkins walked back to her house. Margaret told Sam what the parrot had said about the cat.

Sam listened. For a while he didn't say anything. Margaret knew he was thinking hard. At last Sam said, "Are you sure Polly said a cracked pear seed would fix whatever is wrong with Blackie? That means something *is* wrong with the cat. And we know that the pear seeds are magic." Sam went on thinking. He was quiet all the way to the park.

Prospect Park is very big. It has a lake and a stream and a meadow. There are roads going through the park. Sam and Margaret sat on a fallen tree to eat their lunch. They threw crumbs from their peanut butter sandwiches to a pair of wild ducks who were swimming in the lake. Then they climbed the wooded hill called Lookout Mountain.

Two squirrels were playing tag in a

pine tree. Sam rubbed the pear seed in his pocket and watched the squirrels. After a few moments Sam ran up the trunk of an oak tree. He'd never known how to climb like this before. His hands and feet clung to the bark of the tree. It was easy.

Sam climbed far up into the oak and then took a flying leap to a beech tree nearby. He landed safely on a fat branch and sat down to look around.

Margaret jumped to the lowest branch of the beech tree. From there she climbed to where Sam was sitting. "Isn't it fun, Sam?"

Sam grinned. He stood up on the branch and ran along it to the trunk of the tree. Then he put his arms around the trunk and spun around it.

"I'll race you to the sycamore at the end of the walk." Margaret made a leap to the nearest tree. Sam followed her.

16

MARGARET and Sam chased each other up and down the hills in the park. A woman was walking her dog by the lakeshore. She saw Margaret race up a tree and swing from branch to branch. The woman was so surprised that she slipped into the lake. Sam knew the lake was not very deep, but there were broken bottles and tin cans in it. He ran to help the woman.

After that the twins were careful not to climb the trees when anyone was watching them. They went around the lake and across the meadow. Then they followed a walk that wound over the hills above a little stream. Sam chased Margaret up and down the trunks of a grove of trees. Before they knew it they had come to the entrance to the zoo.

"Oh, Sam," Margaret said, "let's go see the puma they caught in Mrs. Jenkins's yard."

"He must be in the lion house," Sam told her.

"That's the smelliest place in the zoo," Margaret said.

The lion house was crowded. Most of the people were standing in front of the same cage. The cage next to it had a sign *Puma* on it. But there was no sign on the cage with all the people in front of it.

"Nobody knows what that animal is," the keeper was telling the people.

First Sam and Margaret looked at the sleek black puma pacing back and forth in its cage. Then they looked at the big fluffy black cat curled up like a ball in the cage that all the people were watching.

Suddenly Sam made a hissing sound. The black cat lifted its big head and opened its green eyes wide. "Meow," it said in a sad voice.

Margaret had an awful thought. "Sam," she whispered, "that's *Blackie!*"

Sam frowned. "An awfully big Blackie. Mag," he said, "remember the giant angleworm?"

Margaret looked at Sam. Slowly she

began to understand. "It's something about the cave," she said. "It must make things too big. Blackie went into the cave and got to be this size. Then why don't we get too big when we go into the cave?"

"Maybe," Sam said, "it's because we have the magic pear seeds in our pockets."

Margaret pushed her way up to the railing in front of Blackie's cage. "Blackie," she said, "I wish I could help you."

"Meow," the cat said.

Margaret knew that Blackie wasn't used to a cage. He didn't like being shut up in one any more than Polly would. He stretched his big paw through the bars of the cage.

"Get back, little girl!" the keeper warned.

Blackie's paw was turned up as if he

were begging for something. Margaret remembered what the parrot had said. She took one of the pear seeds out of her pocket and cracked it with her thumbnail. She dropped the seed onto the bumpy pads of Blackie's paw.

The keeper grabbed Margaret and pulled her away from the railing. But Margaret had time to see the pear seed pop open. At once Blackie was covered with a thick cloud of gray smoke.

The keeper let go of Margaret. "I'll have to call the fire department," he said.

Everybody was trying to get out of the lion house. Only Sam and Margaret saw the ordinary-sized black house cat crawl out from under the cloud of smoke.

The cat slipped through the bars of the cage and jumped to the railing. Sam picked him up. "Come on, Mag," he said. "We'll take Blackie home."

17

ON the way home the twins didn't play squirrel. They took turns carrying the cat. Blackie purred and purred.

Margaret rang Mrs. Jenkins's bell. The old lady came to the door. Her eyes were very red. She's been crying again, Margaret thought.

Sam handed Mrs. Jenkins the cat. "We found him in the park."

Mrs. Jenkins was so happy that she couldn't say a word. She just held the cat to her face and pressed her cheek against his soft fur.

Margaret and Sam went over to their own house. Elaine let them in. "Mother's lying down," she said. "She has a headache. Polly got into the pantry. She dumped the cornflakes out of the box and overturned a jar of honey. The lid on the honey jar was loose. You never saw such a mess."

"Where is the parrot?" Sam asked.

"She's in my room," Elaine said. "And you're not to punish her, Sam. She doesn't really mean to be bad."

When Mr. Carter came home, the family sat down to supper in the big dining room. Elaine and Mrs. Carter both told stories of Polly's mischief.

"I'm afraid we'll have to get rid of her," Mr. Carter said.

Elaine dropped her fork. "No, no, Daddy. Let's buy a cage for her. We can put a swing in it."

Mr. Carter shook his head. "I like

Polly as much as you do, Elaine. But that bird would never be happy in a cage."

"But we can't get rid of her, John," Mrs. Carter said. "She's a member of the family."

While everyone was talking Joey got up from the table and left the room. A few minutes later the parrot came flapping down the stairs. She flew into the dining room. "Help!" she squawked. "He'll get gravy on my tail feathers."

Joey ran back into the room. "Want to spank Polly," he said.

"I'll be good. I'll be good," the bird screamed. "Just don't let that boy near me."

Mrs. Carter looked at her husband. They both laughed. Polly swung on the light fixture that hung over the dining-room table.

Sam and Margaret waited until supper

was over to talk to the bird. They found the parrot alone in the living room. She was walking back and forth in front of the mirror over the fireplace.

Sam walked over to her and whispered, "Polly, would you like me to crack a pear seed over your head?"

Polly stood still. Her feathers drooped.

Sam reached up and took the bird off the mantelpiece. He looked hard into her face. "Polly," he said, "what do you know about the pear tree magic?"

"That tree is too big," the bird said. "Everything about it is too big. When you dug a little hole under it, it grew into a cave. Now the cave makes everything that comes into it too big."

"Was it the pear seeds that kept us from getting too big?" Margaret asked.

"How did you figure that out?" Polly said. "The pear seeds have much stronger magic than the tree. They've got as much magic as the whole tree crammed into a tiny space."

"And did the seeds help us move like the squirrels?" Sam asked.

"Yes," the parrot said. "That's one of the things pear seeds do. But I can't see why anybody would want to act like a squirrel." The parrot didn't say anything more for a minute. Then, in a very small voice, she said, "Please don't crack a pear seed over me, Sam. I know what it's like to be no bigger than a fruit fly. If I went outdoors I'd be afraid the first bird that came along would eat me. And if I stayed in the house I might be caught by a spider."

Margaret couldn't stand it any longer. "Sam didn't really mean it," she said. "But do be good, Polly."

18

THE following afternoon Margaret went into Elaine's room. She saw the parrot walking around the floor. Polly found a green glass bead and picked it up in her claws. She fluttered up and dropped the bead into a dish on Elaine's dresser. Then she went back to walking on the floor until she found another bead.

Margaret took Elaine's sewing basket out of the dresser drawer. She threaded a needle and sat down on the floor to string the beads. Every time Polly found a bead she brought it to Margaret. When Margaret had strung the last bead, the parrot flew out of the room.

Just then Elaine came upstairs. She was surprised when Margaret handed her the string of beads.

"Thank you, Margaret," Elaine said. "I was just going to pick them up. I broke the string this morning."

"It was Polly who found all the beads," Margaret told her. "I only strung them."

"Polly spent the whole morning helping Mother," Elaine said. "She folded the clothes when Mother took them out of the dryer. And she took a cloth and dusted that high shelf in the dining room that Mother can't reach. Margaret, do you think that bird is sick?"

"Maybe," Margaret said. "I wonder what she's up to now."

The two girls went to look for the parrot. Polly was sitting in the open window of the kitchen. She was talking through the screen to Mrs. Jenkins's cat.

Blackie was on the fence between the yards.

"Meow," the parrot said.

"Meow, meow," the cat answered. He didn't sound angry. After a while Blackie jumped from the fence to the window-sill. He tried to rub his whiskers against the parrot's beak, but the screen was in the way.

Sam walked into the kitchen. "Hey," he said, "those two have made friends. Mag, did you borrow my erector set? I want to show Joey how to build with it."

"I don't have it," Margaret said. "Did you look in your closet?"

Sam scratched his head. "Yes," he said. "But the funny thing is, all I found was the box to the erector set. And it was empty."

Polly had stopped talking to the cat. She flew up to the top of the tall kitchen cabinet. A second later she flew down with one of the metal strips from the erector set. She put it on the kitchen table. Then she flew up and brought down two screws in her claws. The parrot flew up and down until the table was piled with parts to Sam's erector set.

Sam went to get the box. When he brought it down to the kitchen, the parrot helped him put the pieces away.

"Maybe you'd like to help me build a crane, Polly," Sam said.

The bird hopped onto his shoulder. "Sounds like fun," she said.

19

ON Saturday morning the Carters were eating waffles in the kitchen.

"Mrs. Jenkins has such a lovely garden," Mrs. Carter said. "We ought to plant one."

"Well, I bought a spade," Mr. Carter reminded her. "Now, what shall we plant? I can drive over to the garden center on Caton Avenue."

"I'll go with you, John." Mrs. Carter finished her waffle and stood up. "Sam, isn't it your turn to do the dishes?"

"I washed the supper dishes last night, Mom," Sam reminded her. "Elaine dried them. Now it's her turn to wash. Mag can dry. I'll start digging while you and Dad are gone."

Mrs. Carter went to the cupboard on the basement stairs. She took out a brand-new orange trowel and gave it to Joey. "Go help Sam dig up the yard."

Joey took the trowel and ran out into the yard. Sam followed him. Joey dug little holes all around the fence. Sam made a round garden bed in the middle of the yard. Elaine and Margaret finished the dishes and came out to help.

Mr. and Mrs. Carter came back from the garden center with boxes of marigolds and zinnias and asters. They had also bought four rose bushes, one red, one white, one yellow, and one pink.

Everybody worked hard all morning.

The yard began to look like a garden.

"I wish we were planting seeds," Elaine said. "It seems like cheating to stick in plants that are already growing."

"It's too late in the summer to plant seeds," her mother told her. "By the time they were big enough to bloom the frost would kill them. Next year we can plant seeds."

Joey ran into the house and came out with the jar of sunflower seeds. He

started dropping them by the handful into the little holes he had dug along the fence.

Sam took the pear seed out of his pocket. He planted it in the center of the round bed of zinnias before Margaret could stop him.

"Sam," she whispered, "why in the world did you do that? Now we only have one seed left. We'll have to take turns going in the cave."

"I'm not sure I want to go into the cave anymore," Sam said. "Suppose there was a giant pinch bug in there? Anyway I thought I'd plant the pear seed for luck."

There was a sudden rumble of thunder. A few drops of rain began to fall. Mrs. Carter ran to the back door. "Come into the house, everybody," she said. Isn't it lucky? Now we don't have to water the garden."

20

POLLY was so good for the next three days that Margaret decided to give her a treat. "Sam," she said, "we can let Polly fly around outside while we play squirrel."

It seemed like a good time to go into the lot. Mrs. Carter had gone to the supermarket. Elaine was busy sewing a whole new set of buttons on her yellow sweater. Margaret and Sam took the parrot and went out into the yard.

Margaret turned the bird loose as soon as she came out of the back door.

"Last one up the pear tree is a monkey's uncle!" She jumped to the side fence, ran along it to the back of the yard, and leaped into the lot.

Sam came after her. The green bird stretched her wings and flew high in the air. She came down to land on a top branch of a weed tree.

The twins ran up the pear tree, frisking like squirrels. Neither of them wanted to go into the cave.

Margaret climbed to a branch across from where the parrot sat in the weed tree. "Polly, come over here."

The parrot shook her head. "I'd rather not go into that tree," she said. Suddenly the bird caught sight of something on the ground below. She let out a squawk of terror.

Sam and Margaret looked down.

Joey was in the lot! He had found the loose board in the fence and come through. Now the little boy started to push his way through the weeds. In a minute he would come to the cave under the pear tree.

"Stop him! Stop him!" the parrot screamed. "He's bad enough the size he is!"

21

THE twins started climbing down the tree. Margaret thought she'd never get to the bottom. Sam was ahead of her. When he got to the last branch he jumped. He turned his ankle when he landed. "Joey, get back!" Sam yelled.

But Joey had seen the cave. His eyes were shining. "Joey go in," he said.

"No, no!" Margaret called. She knew she could use the last pear seed to make Joey the right size this time. But suppose he came back to the cave again? What should she do? Margaret scraped her legs as she slid down the last few feet of the tree.

Sam tried to stand. He managed to hop over to his little brother. He grabbed Joey's hand.

"Let me go!" Joey slipped out of Sam's

grasp. He started to run toward the cave.

The parrot swooped down. "Quick, a pear seed!" she screamed.

Margaret pulled the last pear seed out of her pocket.

"Crack it!" the bird squawked. "Throw it into that hole you dug . . . and then run!"

Margaret cracked the seed and tossed it into the hole at the foot of the pear tree. She grabbed Joey and carried him to the back fence. Sam half hopped and half ran after her. The parrot flew over their heads.

There was a tremendous crash. The ground seemed to shake. Margaret and Sam pushed Joey through the hole in the fence and crawled in after him. Then they peeked through the fence at the pear tree. It had fallen to the ground and broken to pieces. The cave was gone.

"I'm going to get a hammer and nail this fence board back in place," Sam said.

Margaret was staring at the zinnia bed. "Sam, look!"

Where Sam had planted the pear seed a little tree was growing. It was already six inches high.

Margaret was thinking. "Sam," she said, "at the rate this tree is growing there'll be pears on it before very long —pears with seeds in them."

Sam grinned. "And someday we'll teach Joey to play squirrel in that tree."

"Awk!" said the parrot.